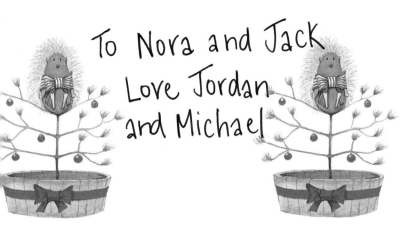

To Nora and Jack
Love Jordan
and Michael

A Porcupine in a Pine Tree Collection

Helaine Becker

illustrated by

Werner Zimmermann

North Winds Press
An Imprint of Scholastic Canada Ltd.

The paintings for this book were created in pencil, ink and watercolour.

Library and Archives Canada Cataloguing in Publication

Title: A porcupine in a pine tree collection / Helaine Becker ; illustrated by Werner Zimmermann.
Other titles: Works. Selections | Porcupine in a pine tree | Dashing through the snow |
Deck the halls
Names: Becker, Helaine, author. | Zimmermann, H. Werner, illustrator.
Description: Includes a song section with sheet music for readers to play along on piano or guitar.
Identifiers: Canadiana 20200194615 | ISBN 9781443175708 (hardcover)
Subjects: LCSH: Christmas poetry. | LCSH: Canada—Juvenile poetry.
Classification: LCC PS8553.E295532 A6 2020 | DDC jC811/.6—dc23

www.scholastic.ca

Music arranged by Trevor P. Wagler.

6 5 4 3 2 1   Printed in China 62   20 21 22 23 24 25

Contents

A Porcupine in a Pine Tree

A Canadian 12 Days of Christmas

On the first day of Christmas,
My true love gave to me:
A porcupine in a pine tree.

On the second day of Christmas,
My true love gave to me:
Two caribou,
And a porcupine in a pine tree.

On the third day of Christmas,
My true love gave to me:
Three beaver tails,
Two caribou,
And a porcupine in a pine tree.

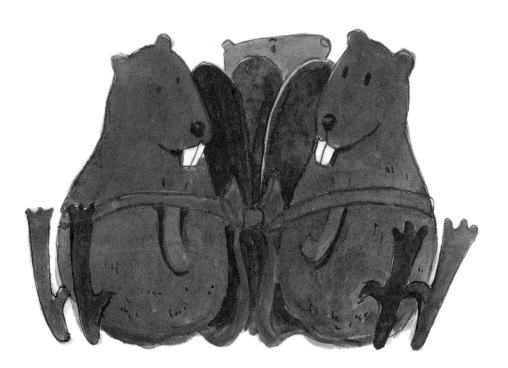

8

On the fourth day of Christmas,
My true love gave to me:
Four calling moose,
Three beaver tails,
Two caribou,
And a porcupine in a pine tree.

10

On the fifth day of Christmas,
My true love gave to me:
Five Stanley Cups,
Four calling moose,
Three beaver tails,
Two caribou,
And a porcupine in a pine tree.

On the sixth day of Christmas,
My true love gave to me:
Six squirrels curling,
Five Stanley Cups,
Four calling moose,
Three beaver tails,
Two caribou,
And a porcupine in a pine tree.

On the seventh day of Christmas,
My true love gave to me:

14

Seven sled dogs sledding,
Six squirrels curling,
Five Stanley Cups,
Four calling moose,
Three beaver tails,
Two caribou,
And a porcupine in a pine tree.

16

On the eighth day of Christmas,
My true love gave to me:
Eight Mounties munching,
Seven sled dogs sledding,
Six squirrels curling,
Five Stanley Cups,
Four calling moose,
Three beaver tails,
Two caribou,
And a porcupine in a pine tree.

On the ninth day of Christmas,
My true love gave to me:

Nine loons canoeing,
Eight Mounties munching,
Seven sled dogs sledding,
Six squirrels curling,
Five Stanley Cups,
Four calling moose,
Three beaver tails,
Two caribou,
And a porcupine in a pine tree.

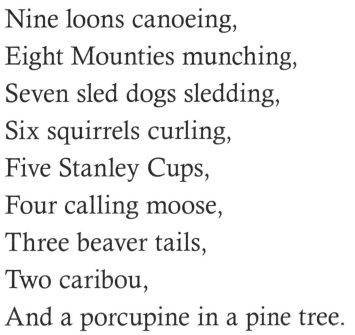

19

On the tenth day of Christmas,
My true love gave to me:
Ten Leafs a-leaping,
Nine loons canoeing,
Eight Mounties munching,
Seven sled dogs sledding,
Six squirrels curling,
Five Stanley Cups,
Four calling moose,
Three beaver tails,
Two caribou,
And a porcupine in a pine tree.

On the eleventh day of Christmas,
My true love gave to me:
Eleven puffins piping,
Ten Leafs a-leaping,
Nine loons canoeing,
Eight Mounties munching,
Seven sled dogs sledding,
Six squirrels curling,
Five Stanley Cups,
Four calling moose,
Three beaver tails,
Two caribou,
And a porcupine in a pine tree.

On the twelfth day of Christmas,
My true love gave to me:
Twelve cubs a-dancing,
Eleven puffins piping,
Ten Leafs a-leaping,
Nine loons canoeing,
Eight Mounties munching,
Seven sled dogs sledding,
Six squirrels curling,
Five Stanley Cups,
Four calling moose,
Three beaver tails,
Two caribou . . .

And a porcupine . . .

. . . in a . . .

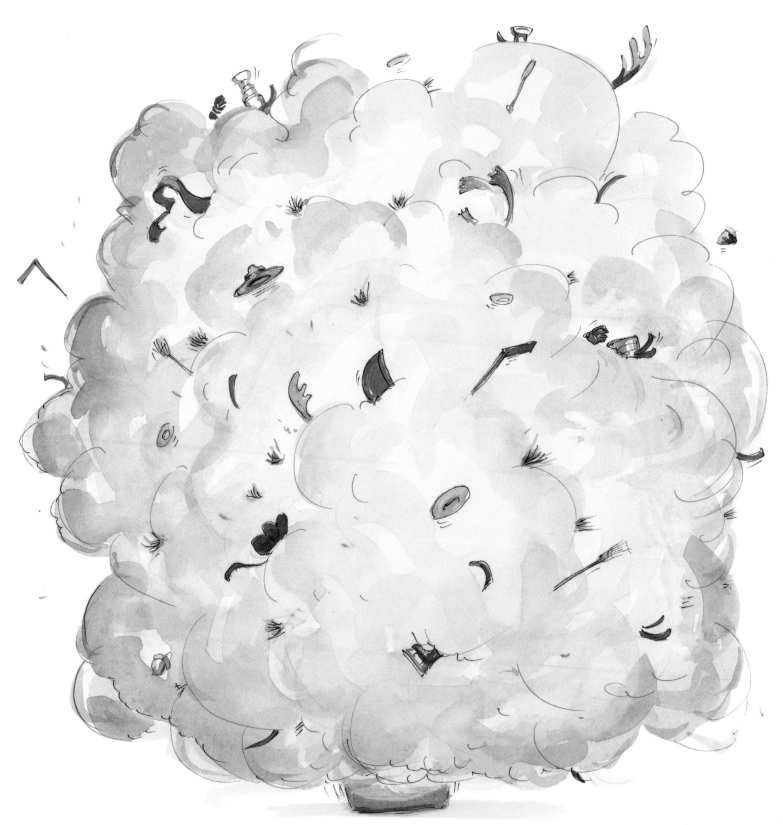

29

PINE TREE!

30

Dashing Through the Snow

A Canadian Jingle Bells

Dashing through the snow,
On a rusty old Ski-Doo,
Through the bush we go,
Dodging caribou.

32

33

Frostbite on my ears,
Nose completely numb,
"Faster, faster!" Beaver cheers,
"For Christmas Eve has come!"

34

Jingle bells, Beaver yells,
"Santa's on his way!"
Oh what fun it is to ride
The jolly True North way, eh?

Jingle bells, Beaver yells,
"Santa's on his way!"
Oh what fun it is to ride
The jolly True North way!

Dashing through the sky,
Across the northern lights,
Santa's soaring high,
Such a thrilling sight.

38

Santa's sled is crammed,
With gifts for everyone,
Sasquatch reaches up a hand
And starts the snowy fun!

41

Jingle bells, Beaver yells,
"Santa's on his way!"
Oh what fun it is to ride
The jolly True North way, eh?

Jingle bells, Beaver yells,
"Santa's on his way!"
Oh what fun it is to ride
The jolly True North way!

43

Spilling from the night,
Gift-wrapped treats for all,
Blizzard of delight,
We duck as presents fall!

Who knows which is which?
Let's open them and see.
You and I should make a switch,
'Cause this one's not for me!

47

Maple candy dish —
What a letdown for this loon!
All she wants is fish,
She steals some from Raccoon.

Owl unwraps a prize,
So does Caribou,
Wouldn't it be wise for them
To make a switcheroo?

49

Fruitcake's quite a treat,
For a nutty otter pup,
Fiddles sound so sweet,
When they're all tuned up!

Muskox gets new boots,
Wolf gets pads — hooray!
They really suit when Wolfie shoots
And scores on Christmas Day.

Jingle bells, Beaver yells,
"Santa's on his way!"
Oh what fun it is to ride
The jolly True North way, eh?

Jingle bells, Beaver yells,
"Santa's on his way!"
Oh what fun it is to ride
The jolly True North way!

Beaver starts the song,
Puffins join right in,
Moose can sing along,
When carolling begins!

It's pins-and-needles time,
Is this the gift for me?
I open it and find it is . . .

A pop-up Christmas tree!

When friendship lends a hand,
Dreams, they do come true!
Have a Merry Christmas and
A Happy New Year, too!

Deck the Halls

A Canadian Christmas Carol

Deck the halls with boughs of holly,
Fa-la-la-la-la, la-la-la-la.
Porcupine is feeling jolly!
Fa-la-la-la-la, la-la-la-la.

Beavers building, busy, busy,
Fa-la-la, la-la-la, la-la-la.

Loons try toe loops and get dizzy!
Fa-la-la-la-la, la-la-la-la.

Don we now our reindeer sweaters,
Fa-la-la-la-la, la-la-la-la.

Muskox like their own coats better!
Fa-la-la-la-la, la-la-la-la.

Caribou in pompom hoodies,
Fa-la-la, la-la-la, la-la-la.

Raid the groaning board of goodies,
Fa-la-la-la-la, la-la-la-la.

Bear cubs gather logs and kindling,
Fa-la-la-la-la, la-la-la-la.

Keep the yule log flames from dwindling,
Fa-la-la-la-la, la-la-la-la.

Round the tree the dogs are racing,
Fa-la-la, la-la-la, la-la-la.

72

Right behind, raccoons are chasing!
Fa-la-la-la-la, la-la-la-la.

'Neath the tree are presents, heaping,
Fa-la-la-la-la, la-la-la-la.

74

Hockey players are a-leaping,
Fa-la-la-la-la, la-la-la-la.

Otters carol, a cappella,
Fa-la-la, la-la-la, la-la-la.

Polar bear's one happy fella!
Fa-la-la-la-la, la-la-la-la.

In the armchair, look who's napping,
Fa-la-la-la-la, la-la-la-la.

Sasquatch is all thumbs at wrapping!
Fa-la-la-la-la, la-la-la-la.

Squirrels curled up by the fire,
Fa-la-la, la-la-la, la-la-la.

Lulled to sleep by
the moose choir!
Fa-la-la-la-la,
la-la-la-la.

81

Drifting into
dream-filled sleep,
Fa-la-la-la-la, la-la-la-la.
Christmas magic, yours to keep,
Fa-la-la-la-la, la-la-la-la.

83

So deck the halls
with boughs of holly,
Fa-la-la, la-la-la, la-la-la.

Make your True North
Christmas jolly!
Fa-la-la-la-la, la-la-la-la!

A Porcupine in a Pine Tree

Traditional

On the first day of Christ-mas, My true love gave to me: A por-cu-pine in a pine tree. On the

sec-ond day of Christ-mas, My true love gave to me: Two car-i-bou, And a por-cu-pine in a pine

tree. On the third day of Christ-mas, My true love gave to me: Three bea-ver tails,

Two car-i-bou, And a por-cu-pine in a pine tree. On the fourth day of Christ-mas, my

true love gave to me: Four call-ing moose, Three bea-ver tails, Two car-i-bou, And a

Dashing Through the Snow

Traditional

1. Dash - ing through the snow, On a rust - y old Ski- Doo, Through the bush we go,
2. Dash - ing through the sky, A - cross the north - ern lights, San - ta's soar - ing high,

Dodg - ing car - i - bou. Frost-bite on my ears. Nose com-plete - ly numb,
Such a thrill - ing sight. San - ta's sled is crammed, With gifts for ev - ery - one,

"Fast - er, fast - er!" Bea - ver cheers, "For Christ-mas Eve has come!"
Sas-quatch reach - es up a hand And starts the snow - y fun!

Refrain

Jin - gle bells, Bea - ver yells, "San - ta's on his way!" Oh what fun it

is to ride The | jol - ly True North | way, eh? | Jin - gle Bells, | Bea- ver yells,

"San - ta's on his way!" | Oh what fun it is to ride The | jol - ly True North way!

3. Spilling from the night,
   Gift-wrapped treats for all,
   Blizzard of delight,
   We duck as presents fall!

   Who knows which is which?
   Let's open them and see,
   You and I should make a switch,
   'Cause this one's not for me!

   Refrain

4. Maple candy dish —
   What a letdown for this loon!
   All she wants is fish,
   She steals some from Raccoon.

   Owl unwraps a prize,
   So does Caribou,
   Wouldn't it be wise for them
   To make a switcheroo?

   Refrain

5. Fruitcake's quite a treat,
   For a nutty otter pup,
   Fiddles sound so sweet,
   When they're all tuned up!

   Muskox gets new boots,
   Wolf gets pads — hooray!
   They really suit when Wolfie shoots
   And scores on Christmas Day.

   Refrain

6. Beaver starts the song,
   Puffins join right in,
   Moose can sing along,
   When carolling begins!

   It's pins-and-needles time,
   Is this the gift for me?
   I open it and find it is . . .
   A pop-up Christmas tree!

   Refrain

7. When friendship lends a hand,
   Dreams, they do come true!
   Have a Merry Christmas and
   A Happy New Year, too!

Deck the Halls

Traditional

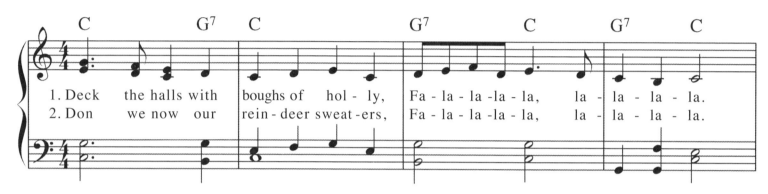

1. Deck the halls with boughs of hol-ly, Fa-la-la-la-la, la-la-la-la.
2. Don we now our rein-deer sweat-ers, Fa-la-la-la-la, la-la-la-la.

Por-cu-pine is feel-ing jol-ly! Fa-la-la-la-la, la-la-la-la.
Musk-ox like their own coats bet-ter! Fa-la-la-la-la, la-la-la-la.

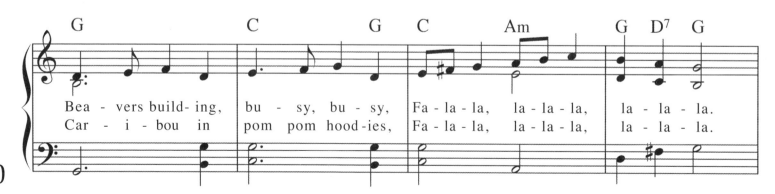

Bea-vers build-ing, bu-sy, bu-sy, Fa-la-la, la-la-la, la-la-la.
Car-i-bou in pom pom hood-ies, Fa-la-la, la-la-la, la-la-la.

90

Loons   try   toe loops | and   get   diz – zy! | Fa - la - la - la - la,   la – | la - la - la.
Raid   the groan-ing | board of   good – ies, | Fa - la - la - la - la,   la – | la - la - la.

3. Bear cubs gather logs and kindling,
   Fa-la-la-la-la, la-la-la-la.
   Keep the yule log flames from dwindling,
   Fa-la-la-la-la, la-la-la-la.

   Round the tree the dogs are racing,
   Fa-la-la, la-la-la, la-la-la.
   Right behind, raccoons are chasing!
   Fa-la-la-la-la, la-la-la-la.

4. 'Neath the tree are presents, heaping,
   Fa-la-la-la-la, la-la-la-la.
   Hockey players are a-leaping,
   Fa-la-la-la-la, la-la-la-la.

   Otters carol, a cappella,
   Fa-la-la, la-la-la, la-la-la.
   Polar bear's one happy fella!
   Fa-la-la-la-la, la-la-la-la.

5. In the armchair, look who's napping,
   Fa-la-la-la-la, la-la-la-la.
   Sasquatch is all thumbs at wrapping!
   Fa-la-la-la-la, la-la-la-la.

   Squirrels curled up by the fire,
   Fa-la-la, la-la-la, la-la-la.
   Lulled to sleep by the moose choir!
   Fa-la-la-la-la, la-la-la-la.

6. Drifting into dream-filled sleep,
   Fa-la-la-la-la, la-la-la-la.
   Christmas magic, yours to keep,
   Fa-la-la-la-la, la-la-la-la.

   So deck the halls with boughs of holly,
   Fa-la-la, la-la-la, la-la-la.
   Make your True North Christmas jolly!
   Fa-la-la-la-la, la-la-la-la!